W9-AMN-842

1109

Here's what kids, parents, and teachers have to say to Ron Roy, author of the A to Z Mysteries series:

"Do you know how much I *love* your A to Z Mysteries? More than 100 ice cream cones!"
—Becca S.

"Your books have changed my reading. Now I love reading."—Bryce.

"I love your A to Z Mysteries so much that I take them everywhere, like in the car, on the couch, and in my room."—Ryan B.

"I read your books over and over again."
—Nina C.

"For the first time ever, [my son] is excited about reading. Thank you for creating books that are so enjoyable and for making reading fun!"—Liz S.

"Thanks for giving [my students] the confidence and love for reading that every child should possess. It was a great year with you in our classroom."—Ria M.

*This book is dedicated to my good friend
Caitlin Lamphier. What a reader!*
—R.R.

To Jesse
—J.S.G.

Text copyright © 2005 by Ron Roy
Illustrations copyright © 2005 by John Steven Gurney
All rights reserved under International and Pan-American Copyright
Conventions. Published in the United States by Random House
Children's Books, a division of Random House, Inc., New York, and
simultaneously in Canada by Random House of Canada Limited, Toronto.

www.randomhouse.com/kids
www.ronroy.com

Library of Congress Cataloging-in-Publication Data
Roy, Ron.
The x'ed-out x-ray / by Ron Roy ; illustrated by John Steven Gurney. — 1st ed.
    p.   cm. — (A to Z mysteries)   "A Stepping Stone Book."
SUMMARY: Ruth Rose, Josh, and Dink attend a concert during which someone
steals the star's diamond pendant, and they are soon on the trail of the thief.
ISBN 0-375-82481-2 (trade) — ISBN 0-375-92481-7 (lib. bdg.)
[1. Robbers and outlaws—Fiction. 2. Musicians—Fiction. 3. Concerts—Fiction.
4. Mystery and detective stories.] I. Gurney, John, ill. II. Title.
III. Series: Roy, Ron. A to Z mysteries.
PZ7.R8139Xed 2005   [Fic]—dc22   2003026515

Printed in the United States of America   10 9 8 7 6 5 4   First Edition

RANDOM HOUSE and colophon and A TO Z MYSTERIES are registered trademarks and
A STEPPING STONE BOOK and colophon and the A to Z Mysteries colophon are
trademarks of Random House, Inc.

A to Z Mysteries®

The X'ed-Out X-Ray

by **Ron Roy**

illustrated by
John Steven Gurney

A STEPPING STONE BOOK™

Random House 🏠 New York

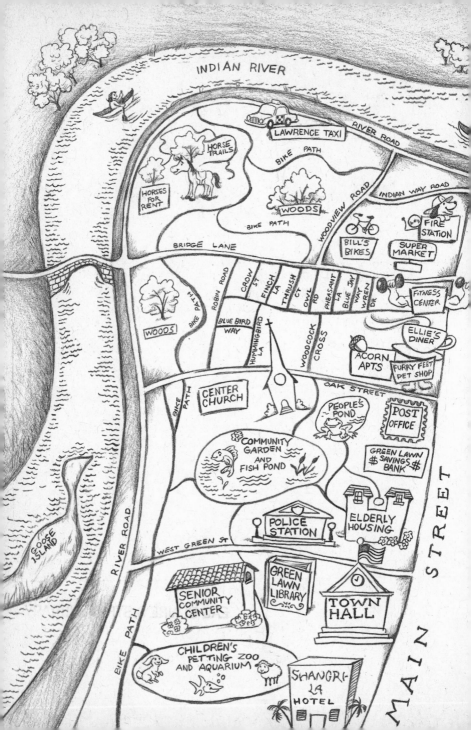

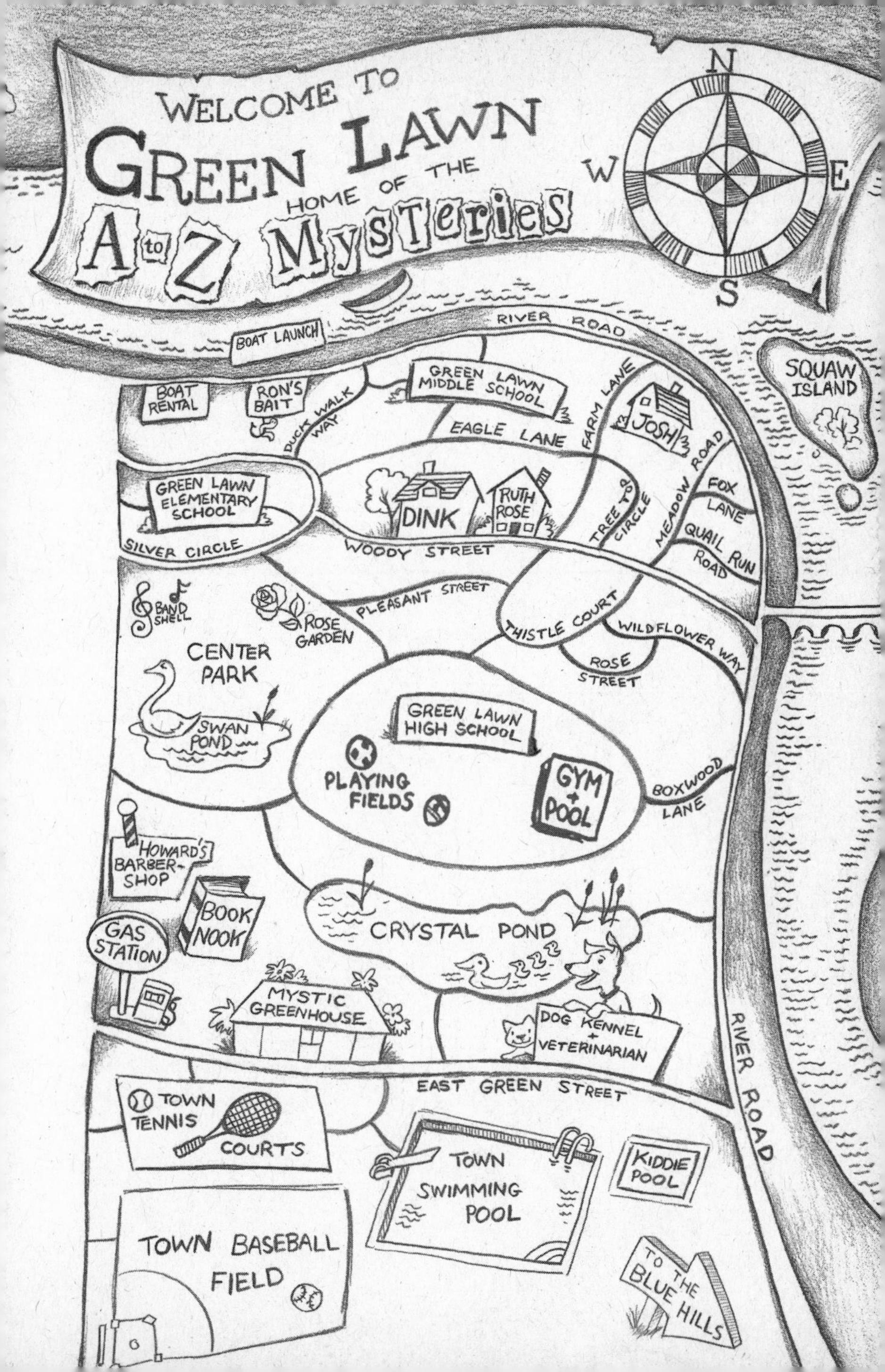
WELCOME TO
GREEN LAWN
HOME OF THE
A to Z Mysteries
N
W
E
S
RIVER ROAD
BOAT LAUNCH
SQUAW ISLAND
BOAT RENTAL
RON'S BAIT
GREEN LAWN MIDDLE SCHOOL
DUCK WALK WAY
EAGLE LANE
FARM LANE
JOSH
MEADOW ROAD
FOX LANE
QUAIL RUN ROAD
TREE TOP CIRCLE
GREEN LAWN ELEMENTARY SCHOOL
SILVER CIRCLE
DINK
RUTH ROSE
WOODY STREET
PLEASANT STREET
BAND SHELL
ROSE GARDEN
THISTLE COURT
WILDFLOWER WAY
ROSE STREET
CENTER PARK
SWAN POND
GREEN LAWN HIGH SCHOOL
PLAYING FIELDS
GYM + POOL
BOXWOOD LANE
HOWARD'S BARBER-SHOP
BOOK NOOK
GAS STATION
CRYSTAL POND
MYSTIC GREENHOUSE
DOG KENNEL + VETERINARIAN
RIVER ROAD
EAST GREEN STREET
TOWN TENNIS COURTS
TOWN SWIMMING POOL
KIDDIE POOL
TOWN BASEBALL FIELD
TO THE BLUE HILLS

CHAPTER 1

"I'm not dressing like a penguin and you can't make me!" Josh said.

"Why not?" asked his friend Dink. "I'm doing it, and so is Ruth Rose."

Dink's whole name was Donald David Duncan. When he was first learning to say his name, it came out as "Dink." That became his nickname.

Josh grinned. "So if you jumped off a bridge, would I have to do it, too?"

"Josh, everyone who goes to a Penelope Gwinn concert dresses like a penguin," Ruth Rose said. "That's because PENGUIN is her stage name."

Ruth Rose always dressed in one color. Today's color was lime green, from her headband down to her sneakers. "Come on, Josh," she went on. "It'll be fun!"

"Eating is fun," Josh said, popping the last of his sandwich into his mouth.

"Penguins like to eat, too," Dink reminded Josh.

"Yeah, raw fish," Josh muttered.

It was Friday, and the kids were in Ruth Rose's backyard having lunch. Ruth Rose had just found out that she'd won four free tickets to Penelope Gwinn's concert in Hartford.

"Be a sport, Josh," Dink said. "All you have to do is wear a white shirt and black pants or shorts. They're passing out penguin masks to everyone who goes."

Ruth Rose gave Josh a sly look. "If you dress up, I'll buy you a hot dog!"

Josh wiggled his eyebrows. "Make it *two* hot dogs and it's a deal," he said.

"Deal," Ruth Rose said. "Be here tomorrow morning at eleven-thirty. My dad is driving us." She started cleaning up the paper plates.

Josh grabbed the last cookie. "Hey, if you throw in a milkshake, I'll even quack like a penguin."

Dink pitched a wadded-up napkin at Josh. "Penguins don't quack," he said. "Only ugly ducklings like you do that."

The next morning, Dink, Josh, and Ruth Rose climbed into her father's station wagon. Ruth Rose was wearing a white T-shirt, a black vest, and white shorts.

"Quick, call a doctor!" Josh teased. "Ruth Rose is wearing two colors!"

Josh's shirt was black with white stripes going up and down. Below the shirt he was wearing black jean cutoffs. White gym socks peeked over the tops of his black high-top sneakers.

"You're supposed to look like a penguin," Dink said, "not a zebra."

"I like stripes," Josh said.

Dink was wearing a black T-shirt and white jeans.

Mr. Hathaway was wearing a white

shirt, a black bow tie, and black trousers. "I don't believe I've heard of Penelope Gwinn," he said as he backed out of his driveway. "What kind of music does she play?"

"Rock and roll," Ruth Rose said. "But she plays a violin while she sings."

"Oh, great," muttered Josh next to Dink in the backseat. "I got dressed like a bird to listen to violin music!"

"You could always stick your two hot dogs in your ears," Dink suggested.

Twenty minutes later, they were in Hartford. Mr. Hathaway parked his car in a lot across the street from Bushnell Park, where the concert was being held.

"Look!" said Ruth Rose, pointing to a white trailer near the park entrance. Painted on the side of the trailer was a life-sized portrait of Penelope Gwinn. On the rear of the trailer was a picture of a real penguin.

"Does she live in that thing?" Josh asked.

"Not a big star like her!" Ruth Rose said. "I think she just travels in it to her concerts. I'll bet she has the penthouse in that hotel!"

Across the street from the park stood the Parkview Hotel. It was twelve stories high, and its windows reflected the blue sky.

"Well, let's find our seats," Ruth Rose's father suggested.

At the gate, Ruth Rose handed the tickets to a man wearing a penguin suit. He told them where to sit, then gave them each a cardboard penguin mask.

"Just fold on the dotted lines to make the beak stick out," the man said. "Then poke out the eye holes so you can see."

The kids and Mr. Hathaway stepped over a lot of feet and legs to get to their seats. Almost everyone was dressed in black and white and wearing a penguin mask.

A tall woman sat in front of Dink. He noticed that she was reading a thick autograph book. Her penguin mask was resting on top of her bright yellow hair.

"I feel like a jerk," Josh said as he placed the mask over his face. His red hair spiked over the top of the mask.

"I think you look very penguin-like, Josh," Mr. Hathaway said as he put on his own mask.

"These are excellent seats!" Dink said. The kids were only twenty feet from the stage. Penelope's band members were all dressed like penguins. They sat at the back of the stage, tuning their instruments.

To the right of the stage was a green tent with a red cross painted over the entrance. Next to the cross were the words FIRST-AID TENT. Several food carts were parked along a path a few yards away.

A police officer on a horse moved

slowly through the crowd. She stopped and chatted with people and let kids pet the horse.

Josh leaned in toward Ruth Rose. "When do I get my hot dogs?" he asked.

"At intermission," she answered.

At exactly one o'clock, the door of the PENGUIN trailer opened up and Penelope Gwinn stepped out. A tall, broad-shouldered man was with her.

Everyone in the audience stood up and started clapping as the star walked across the lawn toward the stage.

Penelope Gwinn was wearing a black-and-white outfit that sparkled. Her black hair was piled high on her head.

Hanging from a chain around her neck was a diamond penguin. The jewel glittered in the sun.

CHAPTER 2

Penelope Gwinn climbed the stage steps, and the crowd settled down.

The tall man stood at the bottom of the steps with his muscular arms crossed.

On the stage, someone handed Penelope her violin. Then the group began to play.

After a few minutes, the band stopped and Penelope Gwinn played her violin. When she began to sing, the audience joined in.

Dink noticed that Josh was snapping his fingers. "Thought you didn't like violin music," he whispered to Josh.

"I don't, usually," Josh said. "But I've never heard anyone play a violin like *this* before!"

Penelope played and sang for about forty-five minutes before she took a break. She handed her violin to a band member and took a deep bow. "Thank you!" she called to the cheering crowd. "I'll be back in twenty minutes!"

The woman in front of Dink pulled her mask down over her face. Then she hurried toward the stage steps with her autograph book.

Josh pulled off his mask and stood up. He grinned down at Ruth Rose. "Those hot dogs smell *so* good!"

Mr. Hathaway handed Ruth Rose some bills. "Lunch is on me," he said. "Meet me back here after intermission."

The kids walked toward the food carts. They passed Presto Pizza and stopped at a cart with a picture of a hot dog on the side. A sign said, FRANK'S FINEST FRANKS.

The man behind the cart was wearing a white jacket. The name "Frank" was stitched in black letters over the pocket.

"I'd like four hot dogs, please," Ruth Rose said.

"Sorry, I'm closing for a few

minutes," the man said. He needed a shave. Dark, curly hair grew on the back of his thick knuckles.

"But I'm starving!" Josh pleaded. He gestured at Dink and Ruth Rose. "My friends are, too."

"Well, all right," the man said. "But make it snappy." He held up an autograph book. "I have to get PENGUIN to sign this for my daughter."

The man pulled two rubber gloves

from a box on his counter. He slipped them over his hands, then plopped four hot dogs into buns and placed them on paper plates. "Drinks?" he asked.

"Three colas," Ruth Rose said. She put her money on the counter.

The man traded the drinks for the bills and slapped down the change. "Mustard and stuff is on the counter!" he yelled as he dashed toward the stage.

"You should get her autograph, too, Ruth Rose," Dink said as he squeezed mustard on his dog.

"I already have it," Ruth Rose said. "When they sent me the tickets, there was a signed picture of PENGUIN in the envelope."

"I hear circus music," Josh said. He pointed toward some trees. "Let's go check it out."

They ate as they walked toward the tall trees.

"A carousel!" Ruth Rose said. "Want to take a ride? Dad gave me enough money."

"No way," Josh said around a mouthful of hot dog. "That's for little kids."

"Come on, Josh," Dink said. "It'll be fun. I haven't been on a carousel for years. Besides, I see some kids our age riding it."

Josh sighed. "Okay, but I'm not sitting on some baby lamb or puppy dog."

The kids finished eating, dropped their trash in a barrel, and hurried to buy tickets. A minute later, the carousel stopped and a bunch of kids hopped off.

Ruth Rose climbed aboard a shiny black horse and sat in its golden saddle. She held on to the safety pole that went from the floor to the carousel's roof.

Dink chose a green dragon with fake red flames shooting from its mouth.

Josh checked out each animal. Finally he chose a roaring lion.

The carousel operator circled the

platform. "Be sure to hold on to your poles," she said. A minute later, the carousel started moving.

Dink held the pole as his dragon moved up and down. He laughed out loud when it suddenly roared and its tail swept back and forth.

He looked for Josh and Ruth Rose. They both waved at Dink.

"My lion is faster than your dragon!" Josh shouted at Dink.

Just then Dink heard yelling from over by the stage. He tried to see what was going on, but a crowd of people blocked his view.

The yelling continued, and Dink still couldn't see. Holding on to his safety pole, he kneeled on the dragon's back for a better view.

But the dragon was slippery, and Dink suddenly felt himself falling. He slid off, landing on the wooden platform.

"Ow!" Dink yelled.

The attendant hurried over. "Are you okay?" she asked, helping Dink to his feet.

"Yeah, but I scraped my arm," he said. "It really hurts."

"Stay right here!" the attendant said. She walked to her lever and stopped the carousel.

Josh and Ruth Rose jumped off their mounts and ran over. "What happened?" Ruth Rose asked.

"I heard someone yelling over by the stage," Dink said. "I kneeled on my dragon to see better and I slipped off."

Josh put his finger on a small swelling on Dink's forehead. "You got a boo-boo," he said, grinning.

"I'm getting my dad," Ruth Rose said, and she took off running.

Just then the attendant came back with a pencil and a pad of paper in her hand. She felt Dink's forehead. "You bumped your head, too," she said. "I'll need your name and address. I have to report all accidents."

While Dink told her, Ruth Rose came back with her father.

"You all right, Dink?" Mr. Hathaway asked.

Dink blushed. "My arm hurts," he said.

Mr. Hathaway checked Dink's arm, then looked at the bump on his head. "I think you'll be fine," he said, "but I'd feel better if you paid a visit to the first-aid tent."

"Good idea," the attendant said. She pointed to a sign: DO NOT STAND ON OR LEAN OFF THE RIDES. "Did you see that sign?"

Dink nodded. "I was trying to see what was going on over by the stage," he said.

"Penelope Gwinn got robbed!" Ruth Rose said.

"What!?" Dink and Josh cried out at the exact same time.

"It's true," Ruth Rose's father said.

As the foursome walked toward the first-aid tent, Josh nudged Dink. "Look at all the cops!" he said.

The stage where Penelope had been singing was surrounded by police officers. The mounted officer was talking to people in the audience. Two other officers were on the stage, standing with Penelope Gwinn. The tall man who had been her escort was nowhere to be seen.

"What did they take?" Dink asked.

"Her diamond penguin," Ruth Rose said. "Someone in a mask snatched it right off her neck!"

CHAPTER 3

Inside the tent, a man was handing a glass of water to a red-faced woman. A boy was standing next to the woman's chair.

"Do you feel better, Mom?" the boy asked.

"Much better, Ronnie," his mother said. "Thank you, Dr. . . ."

"Fleming," the man said, looking down at the tag pinned over the pocket on his white jacket.

She stood up. "Come on, Ronnie, let's get some lemonade," she said to her son. "Thanks again, Dr. Fleming."

"No problem," the doctor said. He glanced up at Mr. Hathaway and the three kids. "Who's the patient?" he asked.

"Me," Dink said.

The doctor pointed to two folding chairs. "Have a seat, please."

There were no other chairs in the tent. "We'll wait outside," Mr. Hathaway said. He guided Josh and Ruth Rose to the tent opening.

"Be a brave little man, Dink," Josh teased.

Dink stuck his tongue out at Josh, then sat down.

"Your name is Dink?" the doctor asked. He pulled two thin rubber gloves from a box and slipped them onto his hands.

Dink nodded. "It's a nickname," he said. "My real name is Donald David Duncan."

The doctor sat in the chair opposite
Dink. He touched the small bump on
Dink's forehead. "How'd this happen?"
he asked.

Dink told the doctor how he fell off
the carousel and showed him the red
scrape on his arm.

"Does it hurt?" the doctor asked.

Dink nodded. "A little, especially when
I twist it."

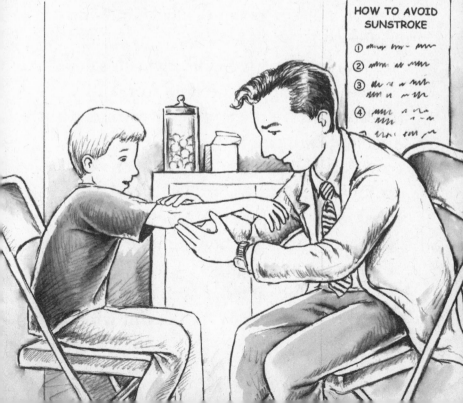

HOW TO AVOID
SUNSTROKE

"Don't twist it," the doctor said.

Just then a police officer stuck his head inside the tent. "Excuse me, Doc," the officer said. "Did you see anyone run by your tent a few minutes ago?"

"Nope, I was pretty busy," Dr. Fleming said. "What's the problem?"

"Someone grabbed Penelope Gwinn's diamond pendant," the officer said. "The perp took off in the crowd."

"Oh no! I hope you catch him," the doctor said.

"Don't worry, we will!" the cop said. "Miss Gwinn might be able to identify the thief, so we're stopping everyone at the main exit gate."

After the police officer left, the doctor turned back to Dink. "Here's what we're gonna do," he said. "I'll bandage your arm, then we'll go to my office and I'll x-ray it."

The doctor pulled a sealed bandage from a white cabinet. "While I'm wrapping your arm, I want you to read that sign over there. Slowly."

Dink looked at the sign. "Why? My eyes are okay," he said.

The doctor opened the package. "I want to make sure you don't have a concussion. Start reading," he said as he began wrapping Dink's arm with the long bandage.

Dink started reading:

HOW TO AVOID SUNSTROKE

1. ALWAYS USE SUNBLOCK

2. WEAR A HAT

3. DON'T STAY OUT IN THE SUN TOO LONG

4. AVOID STRENUOUS EXERCISE ON HOT DAYS

5. DRINK PLENTY OF WATER

"You're a good reader, Dink," the doctor said, finished with the wrapping. "Wiggle your fingers for me."

Dink wiggled his fingers and looked at his arm. The bandage went from his wrist to his elbow. A small metal clip held the end of the bandage in place.

"Not too tight, is it?" the doctor asked.

"No, but the bandage feels weird."

"They always do," the doctor said. "Now we'll call in your father."

"He's my friend's father," Dink explained.

The doctor stepped over to the tent door and invited the others inside.

"How's your boo-boo?" Josh asked.

Dink crossed his eyes.

"I'd like to x-ray Dink's arm in my office," the doctor told Mr. Hathaway. "Can you follow me to the hospital?"

"Of course," Mr. Hathaway said. "You want to leave right now?"

"The sooner the better," the doctor told him, glancing at his watch. "My replacement will be here in a few minutes."

The group left the tent and walked toward the main exit.

Dink noticed an empty space between Presto Pizza and the lemonade stand. Frank and his hot-dog cart had vanished.

At the exit, a line of people stood around mumbling. Two police officers were blocking the closed gate.

The woman with yellow hair who had been sitting in front of Dink was talking to one of the officers. Her face was pale and she looked angry.

"I demand to be let out of this park!" the woman said through clenched teeth.

"Please, you'll all have to stay here just a little while longer," the other officer explained. "We need to wait for Miss Gwinn."

"Come on, follow me," the doctor said. He put his hand on Dink's shoulder and guided him toward the front of the line.

"Hiya, Doc," the officer said. Dink recognized him as the one who had poked his head into the first-aid tent.

"Hello, Officer. Look, I have to get this patient to my office pronto," Dr. Fleming said, his hand still resting on Dink's shoulder. "He has a hurt arm and a possible concussion."

"No problem, Doc," the officer said. He nodded to his partner, who pushed the gate open.

Dink, Josh, Ruth Rose, her father, and Dr. Fleming walked through.

CHAPTER 4

"I'm parked in that lot," Mr. Hathaway said as they crossed the street. "A blue station wagon."

"Me too," Dr. Fleming said. "Mine's a red Jeep. The hospital is about a mile down Main Street."

The kids and Mr. Hathaway followed the red Jeep away from the park and south on Main Street.

"How's that arm?" Mr. Hathaway asked.

"It's okay, thanks," Dink said.

Josh let out a big sigh. "Some people will do anything for attention," he said.

A few minutes later, Dr. Fleming pulled into a small parking lot in front of Hartford Hospital. He parked near a sign that said, HOSPITAL STAFF ONLY.

Mr. Hathaway parked in a visitors' space, and they all climbed out.

Dr. Fleming led the group through a side door and down a long corridor.

They took an elevator to the third floor, then went down another hallway.

Dr. Fleming pushed open a door with X-RAY printed in green letters. Everyone walked in, and Dr. Fleming pointed to some chairs.

"You folks can wait here while I get a couple of X-rays," he said. "This should only take ten minutes or so."

Dr. Fleming led Dink through a door into a smaller room. Pointing to a table covered with a white sheet, he told Dink to lie down. Then he put a lead apron over Dink's chest.

Dink laid his head on a small pillow

and stared up at the ceiling. He could hear Dr. Fleming opening and closing drawers and cupboards. Then Dink saw an X-ray machine slide over the table.

Dr. Fleming's face appeared next to the machine. "Now, I want you to lie very still," he said. He placed Dink's arm across his chest. "When I say 'one,' hold your breath. Let it out when I say 'two.'"

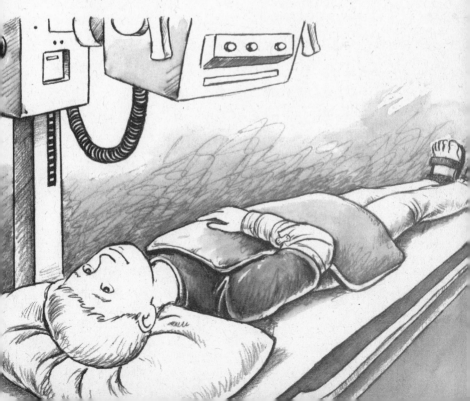

Dr. Fleming's face disappeared. From a few feet away, he said, "One!"

Dink held his breath. He heard something click. Then Dr. Fleming's voice said, "Two! You can breathe now."

Dr. Fleming stepped next to the table again. "I'm going to get a look at this in the other room," he said. "Be back in a jiffy."

Dink counted ceiling tiles until Dr. Fleming returned.

"This shot is too blurred," he said, dropping an X-ray on a table. He grabbed a fat red marker and drew a big X over the X-ray. "I'll have to shoot another one, without the bandage."

Dr. Fleming began removing the bandage from Dink's arm. "See that sign over there?" he asked Dink. "Read it to me, please."

Dink read the sign. It was about drinking milk to make your bones strong.

"There," Dr. Fleming said as he dropped the unrolled bandage on the table next to Dink's shoulder. He positioned Dink's arm again. "Lie still and hold your breath till I tell you to breathe."

Dink did as he was told, and after a minute, Dr. Fleming came back and asked him to sit up. "After I develop this one, you're free to go," he said.

"Okay, this one is much clearer," Dr. Fleming said a few minutes later. "The arm looks fine, but I'll put the bandage back on. No baseball for a few days, okay?"

Dink watched as Dr. Fleming rewrapped his arm. "You should have your own doctor take a look at this," he said.

Then Dr. Fleming opened the door and asked the others to come in.

He showed Mr. Hathaway the X-ray. "No fracture at all," he said. "Probably just strained it when he fell."

"I have to go see my doctor," Dink told Josh and Ruth Rose.

"We should take the X-ray with us," Mr. Hathaway said.

"Of course," Dr. Fleming said. He found a large envelope in a drawer and slipped the X-ray inside.

"Can I have the other one?" Dink asked. "The one that you said was no good?"

"No, I'll just throw . . . sure, why not?" Dr. Fleming said. He slid it into the envelope with the other X-ray and handed it to Dink. "Don't stand up on any more moving carousels," he said.

CHAPTER 5

That evening, Dink ate dinner in front of the TV with his parents. His mother cut his meat for him and made his favorite cookies for dessert. His bandaged arm was resting on a pillow that he held on his lap.

Dink's father winked at him. "Some kids will do anything to get out of their chores," he said.

"Look, there's Penelope Gwinn!" Dink's mother said. She turned up the volume on the TV.

A reporter was interviewing the singer about the theft of her diamond pendant. Dink could see the white PENGUIN trailer behind them.

"It was a gift from someone special," PENGUIN said. "I'm shocked and angry that anyone would steal it."

"I'm sure you must feel terrible," the reporter said. "But your fans feel awful, too. Will you give another concert tomorrow?"

"No, I'm too upset," Penelope said. "I can't think of singing right now, even for

my loyal fans. I'll make sure everyone
gets a refund."

The camera left Penelope's face.

"Well, that's the story," the reporter
said into the camera. "Someone wearing
a penguin mask stole Penelope Gwinn's
priceless necklace while asking her for
an autograph!"

The phone rang. Dink's mother
answered it, then handed the portable
phone to Dink.

"Hello?" he said.

"Did you see that?" Ruth Rose asked. "The thief was one of her fans!"

"I know," Dink said. "Pretty rotten."

Dink stared ahead. He was trying to remember something when Ruth Rose said, "Dink, are you there?"

"Yeah," he said. "Listen, come over tomorrow after I get back from the doctor's, okay?"

Just as Dink hung up, the phone rang again.

"Hello?"

"I think it was that hot-dog guy!" Josh exclaimed. "He had an autograph book, remember?"

"Lots of people there had autograph books," Dink said. Then he remembered something. "Josh? After we came out of the first-aid tent, the hot-dog cart was gone."

"See, I told you!" Josh said. "That guy with the hairy fingers is the thief!"

"*Purloin* means 'to steal,'" he said after a minute.

"Duh," Josh said. "I could have figured that out!"

"Then why didn't you?" Dink asked, grinning at Josh.

"Listen to what Penelope told the reporter," Ruth Rose said, reading the paragraph under the pictures.

I always sign autographs during my intermission. I was signing and thanking my fans when suddenly someone grabbed my necklace. It all happened so fast. Before I could react, the thief was running away.

"We were almost witnesses!" Josh said.

"Except that the necklace didn't get stolen until we were on the carousel," Dink reminded him.

Josh aimed a crooked smile at Dink.

"Actually, only two of us were on the carousel," he said. "You were falling off!"

"I didn't do it on purpose, Josh," Dink said, rubbing his arm.

Ruth Rose was still reading. "It says Penelope stood by the gate as each person left the park," she said. "But she didn't recognize the thief."

"Maybe the guy split right away," Josh said. "He purloined the necklace, then boogied out of the park before they closed the gates."

Dink told Ruth Rose about the missing hot-dog cart.

"You mean it just disappeared?" asked Ruth Rose.

Dink shrugged. "It was gone when we all left the first-aid tent," he said.

"I was right!" Josh said. "Just think, the same fingers that served our hot dogs stole Penelope Gwinn's necklace!"

"Might have," Dink said. "But do you guys remember that woman sitting in front of me during the concert?"

Ruth Rose and Josh shook their heads.

"Well, there was this woman with an autograph book," Dink said. "As soon as Penelope Gwinn announced the intermission, she ran up to the stage. Then when the cops were stopping everyone at the exit, she got all mad at them. Maybe *she* stole the diamond penguin!"

"Penelope never said it was a man," Ruth Rose commented. She glanced back at the newspaper. "She just told the reporter someone stole her necklace."

"So it could have been a man or a woman," Dink said. "Even a tall kid!"

"Maybe Penelope Gwinn remembers something else about the thief today," Ruth Rose said. "She was so upset yesterday, she could have forgotten something important. Why don't we go talk to her?"

"Just like that?" Josh said. "This big star isn't gonna talk to three kids, Ruth Rose."

Ruth Rose grabbed her newspaper. "Well, I think she will. Meet me at my house in five minutes!"

"But I'm hungry!" Josh said. "Don't you people ever eat?"

But Ruth Rose was already out the door.

Dink took Loretta from Josh and put her back in her cage. "Come on downstairs," he said. "Mom made some peanut butter cookies last night."

Josh jumped off the bed. "Finally someone thinks of me!" he said, following Dink out of the room.

Dink found a note on the kitchen table: GONE WITH DAD. BE BACK LATER. —MOM.

Dink turned the note over and wrote a message of his own: GONE WITH JOSH AND RUTH ROSE. BE BACK LATER. —DINK.

He and Josh each ate two cookies with milk. Dink took the last two as they headed out the door.

"Can I have one of those?" Josh asked.

"Oink, oink," Dink said. "These are for Ruth Rose and Nate."

They walked across the lawn to Ruth Rose's house. Dink rang the bell, and Ruth Rose's four-year-old brother, Nate, opened the door.

"Hi, Nate," Dink said, and handed him a cookie.

"Wow, thanks!" Nate said.

He turned and raced away. A minute later, Ruth Rose showed up. She was holding the photograph of Penelope Gwinn with the singer's signature on the bottom.

"When Penelope sees what I wrote on the back, she'll talk to us," Ruth Rose said.

She flipped the picture over. Ruth Rose's note said:

DEAR MISS GWINN,
    WE HAVE INFORMATION ABOUT THE PERSON WHO STOLE YOUR DIAMOND.
    SIGNED,
    RUTH ROSE HATHAWAY,
    DINK DUNCAN, AND JOSH PINTO

CHAPTER 7

"I don't get it," Josh said as Dink handed Ruth Rose the cookie.

Ruth Rose took a bite. "Thanks, Dink. Josh, I think my message will persuade Penelope Gwinn to see us," she explained.

"But what's the information we have?" Josh asked.

"We'll think of something," Ruth Rose said. "Let's go!"

She turned around and yelled into the house, "BYE, MOM. I'M TAKING OFF WITH THE GUYS!"

The kids walked to Main Street and

took a bus to Hartford. They shared a seat toward the rear.

"Well, one thing we can do is describe that hairy hot-dog guy," Josh said. "If he was the thief, she might remember him."

"And I can describe that woman sitting in front of me," Dink said. "They both had autograph books and they were both in a big hurry."

The bus let them off not far from Bushnell Park. "The hotel is on the other side," Ruth Rose said.

They cut through the park, passing by the carousel. The circus music was playing, and a few kids were sitting on the mounts.

"Want to go for a ride, Dink?" Josh teased.

"No, but you can," Dink said. "Or are you afraid to do it alone?"

"I'm not afraid of anything!" Josh said.

"Guys, there's the hotel," Ruth Rose

said and pointed across the street.

They were standing near the stage. The chairs were gone, but the steps up to the stage were still in place.

"Let's check it out," Dink said.

They walked to the stage, passing the first-aid tent. Dink peeked inside. It was empty except for the two chairs and the sign about sunstroke.

Josh climbed up on the stage and gazed out at an imaginary audience. "Maybe I'll become a rock star," he said. "Thousands of people will want my autograph."

Ruth Rose was studying the ground around the stage steps. "Penelope would have come down these steps to sign autographs," she said. "The thief was probably standing right here, waiting for his turn!"

"Or *her* turn," Dink reminded Ruth Rose.

"Or her," Ruth Rose agreed. She bent

over and picked up a small plastic container. "I think this held film for a camera," she said. "I wonder if it's a clue."

Dink picked up a pair of smashed sunglasses. "Come help us search," Dink yelled up at Josh.

"For what?" Josh asked, sitting on the edge of the stage.

"Clues," Ruth Rose said. She held up a dollar bill. "Look what I just found!"

Josh was on the ground in a flash. After searching for five minutes, they had a small pile: the broken sunglasses, the empty film container, a pencil, one dollar, one penny, ten ticket stubs, seven flattened penguin masks, and about a hundred candy wrappers.

They threw the masks, stubs, and wrappers into a trash bin. Ruth Rose put the other stuff in her pocket as they walked toward the hotel.

The trailer was gone.

"What if Penelope isn't even here?" Dink asked. "If she canceled her concerts, maybe she went home. Wherever that is."

"I never thought of that," Ruth Rose said. "We'll know in a minute."

The kids walked into the hotel lobby and up to a long reception counter. Two clerks were standing behind the counter. One was talking on the telephone, so Ruth Rose approached the other one.

"Excuse me, is Penelope Gwinn still staying here?" she asked.

The woman looked at Ruth Rose. "And you are . . . ?"

"I'm Ruth Rose Hathaway," she said. "Penelope Gwinn sent me this signed picture." Then she turned it over so the woman could read the back.

"We were there when it happened," Ruth Rose said. "I think Miss Gwinn would like to hear what we have to say."

The clerk picked up a telephone and dialed a number. "Hello. There are some children in the lobby asking to see Miss Gwinn. They say they have information about the theft of her diamond. Yes, thank you."

The clerk hung up the telephone. "Room 1200, on the twelfth floor," she said. "Elevators are to your right."

The kids found the elevators and got on one. Josh pushed the button for twelve, and they were whisked upward.

When the elevator doors opened, a man was waiting for them. It was the same man Dink had seen escort Miss Gwinn to the stage. He did not look happy to see them.

"I'm Miss Gwinn's manager," the man said. He glared down at the kids with fierce eagle eyes. "What do you have?" His arms were crossed over his broad chest.

"We, um—" Ruth Rose started to say.

"We saw two people who acted weird," Dink said. "We think one of them might be the thief."

Penelope Gwinn walked up behind the man. "Thanks, Hans," she said.

Up close, Penelope Gwinn didn't look like a famous rock singer. She was wearing sweats and her hair was in a ponytail.

"Come inside," Penelope said. She walked into the suite and the kids followed, with Hans right behind them. They were in a large room with a view of Bushnell Park.

"Have a seat, please," Penelope said. The kids sat together on a white sofa.

Hans disappeared through a door.

"Now, tell me more about these two 'weird' people," Penelope said. She sat in a white chair opposite the kids.

Dink described Frank, the man who sold them hot dogs. "He had an autograph book," Dink said. "He told us he had to get you to sign it for his daughter."

"I don't remember him," Penelope said.

"He had really hairy knuckles," Josh added.

"And he left with his cart during intermission," Dink said. "Not long after your necklace got stolen."

Penelope shook her head. "Strange. He'd sell a lot of hot dogs during intermission. Still, I don't recall anyone like that asking for an autograph. And the other one?"

"It was a tall woman with yellow crinkly hair," Dink said. "She had an autograph book, too. As soon as you stopped for intermission, she headed right for the stage. Later, I saw her arguing with the police officers."

Penelope walked over to a small table and pulled open its drawer. "Did either of the autograph books look like this one?" she asked.

CHAPTER 8

She held the autograph book so the kids could see it. "The thief was in such a hurry to get away that he left me holding this," she said.

Penelope Gwinn handed the book to Ruth Rose. It was square, and the word AUTOGRAPHS had been stamped in gold on the dark red cover.

"I don't remember the other two autograph books very well," Dink said. "They were fat like this one, with dark covers, I think."

Ruth Rose studied the book in her hand. "I wonder if the police could get the thief's fingerprints from this," she said.

"I asked about that, but he was wearing gloves," Penelope said.

"That guy at the hot-dog cart wore gloves when he served us!" Josh said.

Penelope shrugged. "Anyone could slip on a pair of gloves," she said.

"Could the thief be a woman?" Ruth Rose asked. "She could have worn gloves to disguise her hands."

"I suppose it's possible," Penelope said. "Everyone was wearing penguin masks, so I didn't really look at faces."

Penelope sighed as she sat down. "Anyone could have grabbed my pendant. As soon as I realized what had happened, I started screaming," she said. "But by then the thief had disappeared in the crowd. Later, I stood by the gate with the officers, but I wasn't able to recognize him or her."

Ruth Rose flipped through the pages.

There were a lot of signatures in the book. The last name wasn't complete.

"I was signing that page when he grabbed my necklace," Penelope said.

Ruth Rose started to hand the book back.

"No, I really don't want the thing," Penelope said. "Do me a favor and drop it in the first trash can you come to!"

Penelope stood up. "I appreciate your coming to see me," she said. She noticed the picture Ruth Rose had brought with her.

"You boys want one of those?" she asked, smiling for the first time.

"Sure!" Josh gushed. "I'm a huge fan!"

Penelope signed two more pictures and gave them to Dink and Josh.

The kids thanked her and left. There was a trash can outside the hotel.

"Are you gonna throw the book away?" Dink asked Ruth Rose.

"No way!" she said.

They sat on a bench and waited for the next bus to Green Lawn. Ruth Rose was reading signatures when Dink poked her and Josh. "Look who's coming this way!"

Penelope Gwinn's manager, Hans, was barreling toward them, wearing wrap-around sunglasses. As he marched down the sidewalk, he kept turning his head, checking both sides of the street.

"Is he after us?" Josh whispered.

"I don't think he sees us," Ruth Rose said.

Suddenly Hans stopped in front of a store window. He peered through the glass, then opened the door and disappeared inside.

A sign on the window said: YE OLDE JEWELRY SHOPPE. WE BUY AND SELL UNUSUAL ITEMS.

"Oh my gosh!" Ruth Rose said. "Maybe Penelope's manager is the thief. He could be in there selling the penguin right now!"

"He'd have to be pretty dumb to sell the thing on the same street where he just stole it," Dink said.

"Or maybe he's pretty smart," Josh said. "He could be selling it here because no one would expect him to do that! I wondered why Hans didn't stop the thief. Wasn't he standing at the bottom of the stage steps?"

"That's a good question," Ruth Rose

said. "Should we follow him into the shop?"

"I don't think so," Dink said. "If he went in there to sell the pendant, he'll stop when he sees us walk in. Plus, then he'll know we suspect him."

"So what should we do?" asked Josh.

"I don't know," Dink said. "We can't accuse Hans just because he walked into a jewelry store. And we can't accuse that woman I saw, or Frank the hot-dog man. The thief was wearing a mask and didn't leave any clues behind!"

"Just this," Ruth Rose said as their bus came along. She held up the red autograph book.

A half hour later, the kids were back in Dink's room. While Dink fed Loretta, Ruth Rose read the rest of the pages in the autograph book.

Josh was prowling in Dink's things, looking for candy. "Hey, what's this?" he asked, holding up Dink's souvenir X-ray.

"That's one of the X-rays the doctor took yesterday," Dink said.

"Why does it have this big *X* over it?" asked Josh.

Dink explained that the X-ray was blurred because of the bandage. "He took a second X-ray with the bandage off."

"Guys, look at this!" Ruth Rose suddenly exclaimed. She had the autograph book opened to the inside back cover. "Listen—*To Georgie from Aunt Alva Horst, Christmas, 1980.*"

"The thief's name is Georgie?" Josh asked. He was holding Dink's X-ray up to the window.

"Well, now we know it wasn't the hot-dog man," Dink said. "His name is Frank."

"How do you know that?" asked Josh.

"Because *Frank* was stitched over the

pocket of his jacket, Josh," Dink replied.

"But Georgie could have been wearing Frank's jacket while he stole the necklace!" Josh exclaimed.

"Josh is right," Ruth Rose said. "Or this book could belong to that woman, Dink. Georgie could be a woman's name."

"Yuck, it comes off," Josh said.

Dink looked up to see Josh rubbing something red on the X-ray.

"Josh, what are you doing?" Dink asked. "Don't ruin that X-ray."

"I'm not ruining it," Josh said. "This red marker stuff is coming off on my fingers."

Josh used his T-shirt to wipe away the rest of the red X. "Look at this," he said.

Where the two lines of the X had crossed each other, Dink, Josh, and Ruth Rose could now see a funny shape. It looked like a fuzzy egg, or a pear.

"What is it?" Ruth Rose asked.

"I don't know," Dink said. "But whatever it is, that doctor covered it up with that big *X*."

CHAPTER 9

The kids held the X-ray up to Dink's window and examined the weird shape from all angles.

Ruth Rose traced around the shape with her finger. "It looks kind of familiar. . . . OH MY GOSH!" she yelled. "Dink, go get the morning newspaper!"

Dink raced out of the bedroom and was back half a minute later with the paper.

Ruth Rose found the picture of Penelope Gwinn and the drawing of the stolen pendant. "If I'm right . . ."

Ruth Rose held the drawing of the

pendant to the glass of Dink's window. Then she placed the X-ray on top of the newspaper page. The funny shape they had been trying to identify fit over the pendant. The drawing was a little bigger than the shape on the X-ray, but they were the same.

"The blurry shape is a penguin!" Ruth Rose shouted. "It's exactly like Penelope Gwinn's!"

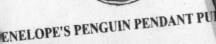

"I don't get it," Dink said. "How could Penelope's pendant be on this X-ray?

Josh looked at him. "You tell us," he said. "It's your arm in the X-ray."

"Dink, what happened in the first-aid tent?" Ruth Rose asked. "What did the doctor do?"

Dink thought back to yesterday morning. "He wrapped my arm, then he took me to the . . . no! Wait a minute! While he was putting the bandage on my arm, he made me read a sign taped to the tent wall!" he said.

Dink looked at Josh and Ruth Rose. "He said he wanted me to read to make sure I didn't have a concussion," Dink went on. "But I think that doctor stole the pendant! He hid it inside the bandage and made me read so I wouldn't see him do it!"

"But why would he put it inside your bandage?" Josh asked.

"I know," Ruth Rose said. "He knew

the cops might be searching people, so he hid it on you. He let you sneak the pendant out of the park for him."

Dink nodded, feeling his heart racing. "Then, when he got me to the X-ray office, he unwrapped the bandage and took the pendant out."

"But didn't you see him do that?" Josh asked.

Dink shook his head. "I was so dumb," he said. "He had me read another sign while he was taking the bandage off! I wasn't looking at my arm!"

"So the thief wasn't the hot-dog guy," Josh said. "Or that woman or big Hans. It was your doctor!"

"How do we find him?" Ruth Rose asked.

"His name is Dr. Fleming," Dink said, remembering the name tag.

"Georgie Fleming," Josh said, looking at the autograph book.

"Let's call Hartford Hospital," Ruth

Rose suggested. "How many Dr. George Flemings could there possibly be?"

They ran to the telephone in the hallway. Ruth Rose got the number for the hospital and dialed. There was no Dr. George Fleming on their staff. No Georgette or Georgina or Georgia, either. No G. Flemings at all.

But there was a Dr. Richard Fleming.

"May I speak to him?" Ruth Rose asked. A minute later, she was talking to Dr. Richard Fleming.

She asked him two questions: Was he working in the first-aid tent in Bushnell Park yesterday? Did he know anyone named Georgie Fleming?

Ruth Rose hung up. "He was home with a cold yesterday," she said. "And he's never heard of Georgie Fleming."

"Great," said Dink. "So how do we find the Dr. Fleming who was in the tent yesterday?"

"Dr. Richard Fleming told me something else," Ruth Rose said with a little grin on her face. "Someone stole his white jacket yesterday. Right out of his office!"

Dink and Josh just stared at her.

"With his name tag on it," Ruth Rose added.

"So . . . so if the guy in the tent wasn't Dr. Fleming, who was he?" Dink asked.

"He was Georgie, the thief!" Josh said.

"But he knew doctor stuff," Dink said. "He took me to the hospital and x-rayed my arm."

"Maybe he *is* a doctor, just not Dr. Fleming," Ruth Rose suggested.

"Then why would he need to steal some other doctor's jacket and name tag?" Dink asked.

"If he knew he was gonna snatch that diamond," Josh said, "he wouldn't wear his own name."

Dink nodded. "That makes sense. But who is he? Where does he live?"

"Georgie knows his way around Hartford Hospital," Josh said. "So maybe he lives in Hartford." He pointed at the autograph book. "And if he lives in Hartford, maybe his aunt Alva Horst does, too!"

Josh picked up the telephone and dialed Information. He was given a phone number for A. Horst, and he dialed it.

When a woman answered, Josh asked if he was speaking to Alva Horst.

When she said yes, he told her that he had found an autograph book belonging to Georgie with her name in it.

"Could you give me his name and address so I can send it to him?" Josh asked.

Georgie's aunt supplied his name and address, and Josh hung up. "His name is George Shill," he told Dink and Ruth Rose. "He lives on Laurel Street in Hartford."

CHAPTER 10

"We can't just show up at the guy's house," Josh said. "He'd just deny the whole thing."

"But we have this X-ray for proof," Dink said. "And that autograph book."

"Get real, Dink. We're kids and he's a grown-up," Josh said. "He'll just tell us to get lost."

"I know one person he won't tell to get lost," Ruth Rose said as she reached for the telephone.

Twenty minutes later, Officer Fallon was sitting in Dink's living room.

The kids told him the whole story.

"I'm glad you called me," Officer Fallon said. "George Shill might still have the pendant. He hasn't had much time to get rid of it."

He placed a call to the Hartford chief of police. They agreed to meet near Georgie's house in forty-five minutes.

"Dink, you should come along to identify this guy," Officer Fallon said. "Are your folks home?"

"They went out," Dink said. "But I could leave them a note telling them I'm with you."

Dink looked at Josh and Ruth Rose. "Could they come, too? They solved the mystery," he said.

Officer Fallon grinned. "Sure, we'll all go," he said. "I wouldn't want to break up the gang!"

Two Hartford police cruisers were waiting when Officer Fallon pulled up to the corner of Laurel Street.

The kids waited in the backseat as Officer Fallon talked with the Hartford officers.

"You ready, Dink?" Officer Fallon asked when he came back to his cruiser.

Dink nodded. His stomach was flipping like a fish on a line.

"Let's go," Officer Fallon said. "The other guys will be around back, in case Georgie decides to leave that way."

Officer Fallon drove slowly up Laurel Street and stopped at number 13. The house was old and made of brick. One shutter was hanging crooked and the lawn needed mowing. All the shades were pulled down.

Officer Fallon and Dink walked up to the door. Dink was holding the envelope with the X-ray inside. His legs felt like cooked spaghetti.

The man who answered the door was wearing jeans and a T-shirt. He was barefooted and eating a doughnut, but Dink recognized him. It was the "doctor" who had been in the first-aid tent the day before. "It's him," Dink whispered.

"Mr. Shill, is it?" Officer Fallon said.

George Shill swallowed nervously. "What . . . who . . . ?"

Officer Fallon held out the autograph book. "Did you lose this?"

Georgie looked at the book. "I . . . I think so. Where did you find it?"

"Penelope Gwinn had it," Officer Fallon said. "She was signing it for you when you grabbed her diamond pendant yesterday. Then you hid the jewel in this boy's bandage so you could sneak it past the cops in Bushnell Park. You removed it at the hospital when you took X-rays."

George Shill nearly dropped his doughnut. His mouth opened and shut, but no words came out.

"Nothing to say, Mr. Shill? Or should I call you Dr. Fleming?" Officer Fallon said. "Maybe *this* will help you find your tongue."

Officer Fallon nodded to Dink, who held up the X-ray.

"Mr. Shill, if I searched your house, would I find Miss Gwinn's pendant?" Officer Fallon asked. "Would I find the jacket you stole from Dr. Fleming's office?"

Georgie found his voice. "I—I can explain everything," he stammered.

"Yes, I'm sure you can, but let's save it till we get to the station," Officer Fallon said, pulling out his handcuffs.

Officer Fallon handed Georgie over to the Hartford cops. Then, with the pendant safe in his shirt pocket, he drove the kids to the Parkview Hotel.

Officer Fallon parked, then pulled the diamond penguin and its chain from his pocket. He passed it over to the backseat. "I called ahead, and she'll be waiting in the lobby."

Dink took the pendant and the kids walked into the lobby. Penelope Gwinn and her manager were sitting together.

"Here, you should give it to her," Dink said, handing the pendant to Ruth Rose. "You found Georgie's name in the autograph book."

Ruth Rose took the pendant, then she gave it to Josh. "You figured out how to find him," she said. "Go ahead, Penelope is waiting."

Penelope Gwinn and Hans stood up and smiled. Josh gulped and handed the diamond penguin to Penelope.

"Thank you so much!" she said. "How did you ever find it?"

"We found a name inside the autograph book," Ruth Rose explained. They told the whole story, and Dink showed her the X-ray.

Officer Fallon was on his telephone. He hung up and stepped forward. "Georgie Shill got tossed out of medical school for cheating on exams," he said. "And that wasn't the first time he'd been in trouble. Anyway, he read about your concert, Miss Gwinn, and he decided to be there. He used the autograph book to get close enough to steal your pendant."

Penelope handed the pendant to Hans, who fastened it around her neck.

"Georgie went to the first-aid tent and told the medical student on duty that he was needed back at the hospital," Officer Fallon went on. "Of course, Georgie was wearing Dr. Fleming's stolen jacket and name tag, so the other guy believed him. After that, Georgie just waited for your intermission."

Penelope smiled. "That pendant means a lot to me," she said. "Hans gave it to me when we were married."

Josh gaped at the big, fierce-looking manager. "He's your husband?" Josh asked. "We saw him go into a jewelry shop. He looked all sneaky, so we thought he might have been the thief!"

Penelope poked her husband. "Why

were you sneaking into a jewelry store?" she asked.

Hans grinned. "I was trying to buy you a new penguin pendant," he said.

Penelope gave him a kiss. Then she kissed Dink, Josh, and Ruth Rose.

A to Z Mysteries

Dear Readers,

I hope you enjoyed reading *The X'ed-Out X-Ray*. It was a lot of fun to write. Many of you ask if my stories are taken from real life. Yes, parts of these stories do come from things that happened to me or to people I know. Here's one example:

When I was Dink's age, I once climbed up on a neighbor's garage to watch his dad do some repair work. When my mom called me for lunch, I made the mistake of jumping down to the ground! I landed on my right arm instead of my feet, and my arm broke. I was in a cast for several weeks! This gave me the idea to have Dink hurt his arm, and the rest of the story came along after that.

I think most writers get ideas from real-life situations. But we also make up a lot—that's why these books are called fiction. I am also asked if I know real kids named

Dink, Josh, and Ruth Rose. Nope. I made them up, but I have to admit that when I created Dink I was thinking

Leslie and John Flynn

about myself at his age. In fact, when I was in college, *my* nickname was Dink!

I can't believe that I have almost reached the end of this series. What a thrill! I hope you will read and enjoy my new series, CAPITAL MYSTERIES. You can read about the two main characters—KC and Marshall—on my Web site, www.ronroy.com.

Bye for now, and keep on reading!

Sincerely,

Ron Roy

P.S. Here's a great picture of sister and brother A to Z fans Leslie and John Flynn.

Collect clues with Dink, Josh, and Ruth Rose
in their next exciting adventure,

THE YELLOW YACHT

Suddenly a shrieking whistle drowned out all the other sounds. It was coming from the bank building. As Dink, Josh, and Ruth Rose watched, the bank door opened and a man burst outside. When he noticed Sammi and the kids, he rushed over.

"Sammi, you must get your father!" the man said. "Immediately!"

"Mr. Silk, what's wrong?" Sammi asked.

"The vault has been robbed!" he said. "The king's gold is gone!"

Track down all these books for a little mystery in your life!

A to Z Mysteries®
by Ron Roy

Capital Mysteries
by Ron Roy
Who Cloned the President?
Kidnapped at the Capital
The Skeleton in the Smithsonian
A Spy in the White House

The Case of the Elevator Duck
by Polly Berrien Berends

Ghost Horse
by George Edward Stanley

Check out Ron Roy's brand-new series about KC and Marshall in Washington, D.C.!

Capital Mysteries

When the President of the United States starts acting funny on TV, KC decides he's not the *real* President Thornton. She's sure he's a clone!

KC's mom and President Thornton have disappeared during the Cherry Blossom Festival. They were kidnapped—right under the bodyguards' noses!

Leonard Fisher claims he's the heir to the Smithsonian fortune. If KC and Marshall can't prove he's a liar, Washington will lose its world-famous museums!

KC's mom is marrying the President of the United States, or is she? The wedding may be canceled because someone keeps leaking the secrets!